DATE DUE

AUG 13 '92	OCT 08 '97		
DE 11 '92	SEP 23 '98		
MY 27'93	AG 16 00		
	AG 18 '05		
JE 30'93	OC 01 07		
JY 2'93	JY 14 11		
FEB 24 '96	AG 10 '11		
JUL 03 '96	28 11		
JUL 13 '96			
AUG 14 '96	AP 03 15		
MAR 10 '97			
JUL 07 '97	17 '22		

Why, Charlie Brown, Why?

A Story About What Happens
When a Friend is Very Ill

created by
Charles M. Schulz

introduction by Paul Newman

TOPPER BOOKS
AN IMPRINT OF PHAROS BOOKS • A SCRIPPS HOWARD COMPANY
NEW YORK

WHY, CHARLIE BROWN, WHY? was developed in cooperation with the American Cancer Society, with special thanks to the California Division, American Cancer Society and Sylvia Cook, R.N.,Stanford Children's Hospital.

Library of Congress Cataloging-in-Publication Data
Schulz, Charles M.
Why, Charlie Brown, why? : a story about what happens when a friend is very ill / Charles M. Schulz.
p. cm.
Summary: The members of the Peanuts gang have varying reactions when they learn that their friend Janice has leukemia and they follow her treatment and ultimate recovery.
ISBN 0-88687-600-1 : $7.95 pb
0-88687-601-X : $12.95
[1. Leukemia—Fiction.] I. Title.
PZ7.S38877Wk 1990 89-43223
[E] —dc20 CIP
AC

Printed in the United States of America

Topper Books
An Imprint of Pharos Books
A Scripps Howard Company
200 Park Avenue
New York, NY 10166

10 9 8 7 6 5 4 3 2 1

Having cancer is a fact of life for kids like Janice in WHY, CHARLIE BROWN, WHY? Janice has leukemia, which is a form of cancer. Having cancer can make you feel different from other kids.

At The Hole In The Wall Gang Camp in Ashford-Eastford, Connecticut, there are many children like Janice. Our camp is a place where kids with cancer and serious blood diseases can go and not feel different. Children of all ages come from around the United States, and everyone there is in the same boat. Sometimes a camper has to take time out for a treatment or medication but, as much as possible, The Hole In The Wall Gang Camp is like a regular overnight camp, with swimming, crafts, campfires—the whole nine yards.

When a child has cancer, it's a difficult time for everyone. Certainly it's difficult for the child herself. But it's also hard on friends and siblings. Sometimes it's hard to understand why a sick brother or sister is getting more attention, or a classmate who is having chemotherapy doesn't have to do extra homework. You can understand it in your head but sometimes it's hard to understand in your heart.

And that's what this book is about, understanding. It's about understanding why your sister or brother might need more attention than you do... or why your schoolmate is allowed to skip assignments.

But understanding is also a fact of life. And in WHY, CHARLIE BROWN, WHY? you'll read about how Charlie Brown, Linus, and the rest of the Peanuts gang start to understand a little about cancer and a whole lot about life.

Best personal wishes,

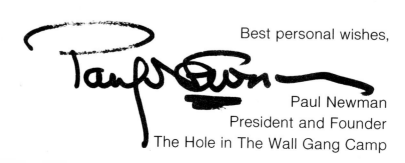

Paul Newman
President and Founder
The Hole in The Wall Gang Camp

*I*t was a beautiful cool, clear autumn morning, just chilly enough so that the children waiting for the school bus were wearing their jackets. Charlie Brown's sister, Sally, was complaining, as usual.

"Some day there will be a monument right here, and you know what it will say? It will say, 'Here is where Sally Brown wasted the best years of her life, waiting for the school bus.'"

Linus was talking with Janice, a little girl with beautiful blonde hair who had moved into the neighborhood several months ago. She sat behind Linus in class.

"Did you enjoy the swings yesterday, Janice?"

"I sure did," said Janice. "I love the swings, and you are the best swing pusher in school."

"Well," said Linus, "it's fun pushing you because you go higher than anybody else."

Charlie Brown's dog, Snoopy, was hanging around with them, of course, and when the school bus finally pulled up to the curb, he was the first one to jump in.

Unfortunately, the driver booted him out immediately.

"Sorry," explained Charlie Brown. "You can't go with us. Dogs aren't allowed on the school bus."

"Woof," said Sally.

Snoopy was not about to get left behind, though. He hurried around to the rear of the bus and jumped up onto the back bumper, where he happily played his harmonica.

As Janice climbed the steps into the bus, she bumped her elbow on the railing. "Ow," she groaned. "Great! Now I'll have another bruise."

She held her arm out to show Linus. "Look, I bumped myself last week and the bruise is still there. Look at all the bruises on my legs."

"You do have a lot of bruises."

"I know," said Janice. "I feel so clumsy."

When the children got off the bus and walked onto the school grounds, Linus asked Janice if she would like to be pushed on a swing before they went in.

"I don't think so, Linus," she said. "I'm not sure I feel well today, but thank you anyway."

"Is it your stomach?" asked Linus. "Maybe it's just nerves. I always get a stomachache when I know we're going to have a test."

Janice shrugged. "Maybe."

Later, even after they were seated at their desks, Janice still did not seem herself. Linus asked, "Are you all right?"

"I don't know," replied Janice. "I've just been feeling so tired lately. Feel my head, will you, Linus? Is it warm? I think I may have a fever."

He reached back and felt her forehead with the palm of his hand. "Yes," he said. "It is a little warm. If you don't feel well, maybe you should go see the nurse."

"I guess I should," she said. So just before class started, Janice got up from her desk and walked slowly across the room, out the door, and down the hall to the nurse's office. There, her temperature was taken by the nurse and found to be 102 degrees. Janice agreed that she should call her mother to come and pick her up to take her home. In the meantime, her homeroom teacher asked Linus what he had been talking about with Janice.

"Well, ma'am," he said. "She wasn't feeling well, so I told her she should go see the nurse...No, ma'am, I'm not a doctor."

Several days went by, the weather grew a little colder, and the children found themselves waiting for the school bus without Janice.

"I don't know, Charlie Brown," said Linus. "I haven't heard a word from her since the day she went to see the school nurse."

As usual, Sally was complaining. "Why does everyone worry so much about Janice? I'm the one who's going to have a bad day."

"Why is that?" asked Charlie Brown.

"Because I left my lunch sitting on the curb."

This was, of course, just the sort of break Snoopy waited for. As a dog, he felt that anything left behind belonged to him and in no time at all, he was enjoying a wonderful early morning snack.

That morning, Linus's teacher was finally able to explain to everyone why Janice had not returned to class. Janice was in the hospital. She would not be returning to school for a while. After school let out in the afternoon, Charlie Brown and Linus, being very thoughtful, decided to visit their friend. They were a little surprised to see Snoopy walking down one of the hospital corridors dressed as the world famous surgeon. Of course, they had long ago become used to his strange actions. They were slightly puzzled, however, when they saw him running furiously up and down several flights of stairs.

"Why is the world famous surgeon running up and down the stairs like that, Charlie Brown?"

"I imagine it's because he can't reach the elevator buttons."

The two boys found Janice's room. She was delighted to see them.

"Our teacher told us you were in the hospital," said Linus. "Your fever must have been awful."

Janice held up her arm. An I.V. needle was attached to it. "It wasn't just a fever," she said. "I have cancer."

"Cancer?" exclaimed Linus. "I don't understand. How do they know that?"

"Well," said Janice, "they've done lots of tests on me. They found out that I have leukemia. That's why I had all those bruises. My blood has cancer in it."

"You're not going to die, are you?" asked Charlie Brown.

"Good grief!" said Linus. "What kind of a question is that?"

"That's all right," said Janice. "I asked the doctors the same question. They took several blood tests and I even had a bone marrow test. Leukemia cells live deep inside my bones where blood is made. They stuck a needle right here into the bone to take some marrow out."

"Oh, no!" said Linus. "That must've hurt a lot!"

"Well, yes," said Janice. "I guess it did, but first they numb your skin, and anyway, it didn't last long. Now they have me hooked up to this intravenous. It's a way of giving me chemotherapy. This medicine will probably help me, but they tell me it could also make my hair fall out. Please don't worry. I know I'm going to get well because I want to get back to school and swing on those swings."

"You get well, Janice," said Linus, "and I'll push you on those swings forever."

It was early evening as the boys walked slowly home. A lot had happened to them in their short lives, but this was the first time they had ever faced anything serious. Linus, especially, felt an ache within himself unlike anything he had ever known. He realized how much Janice meant to him as a friend, and the more he thought about it, the less he felt he could understand what was happening.

As they paused before leaving each other, Linus turned and said, "Why, Charlie Brown, why?"

This time, Charlie Brown had no answer, and Linus walked slowly away.

When Linus got home, his sister, Lucy, was sitting in front of the TV set.

"Charlie Brown and I were visiting Janice in the hospital," he said. "She has leukemia."

"While you're up," said Lucy, "why don't you get me a glass of milk?"

Linus turned quickly, went to the kitchen, poured the milk for Lucy, and brought it to her. "I remember that day," he said, "when she wasn't feeling well. I remember touching her forehead and feeling how warm she was."

"You touched her forehead?" shouted Lucy. "And now you're handing me a glass of milk? You could catch leukemia from her and give it to me!"

"Cancer is not contagious," said Linus. "You can't catch it from somebody like a cold or flu."

"She probably got it," said Lucy, "because she's a creepy kid."

"Janice did not get cancer because of something she did wrong. It just happened."

"Well, anyway," said Lucy, handing the glass to Linus, "take the milk back."

"No, thank you," said Linus. "I don't want to catch your crabbiness!"

Autumn turned quickly into winter that year, and soon the streets were covered with snow. A huge snowplow worked the roads near where the children were waiting that morning for the daily school bus. It turned out to be a very special morning, for Janice suddenly appeared, wearing a new pink cap.

"You're back!" cried Linus, barely containing his glee. "You've been away from school for a long time. Is everything okay? Are you better now?"

"Well, I think I'm getting better," replied Janice. "My doctor says I'm doing great."

When the bus arrived, they boarded together.

"They've put the swings away for the winter," said Linus. "I'm sorry. I was looking forward to giving you a good push on the swings."

"That's all right," said Janice. "There'll be another time for that."

When they got to school, an obnoxious-looking boy ran up and shouted, "Hey, nice hat! Pretty cute! Does it fly? I think it needs a propeller," and he reached up and knocked the pink cap from Janice's head. Janice tried to cover her head with her hands, but it was too late. Everybody on the playground, including Linus, saw that her hair was gone.

"Hey, look at this!" the obnoxious boy shouted. "Check it out! A baldie!"

Tears filled Janice's eyes. When Linus saw this, all of the emotion that had been building up inside him came pouring out, and he shouted furiously at the obnoxious kid, "What's the matter with you? Huh? What's the matter?"

"What's the matter with me?" shouted the kid. "What's the matter with her? She's bald! She's got no hair!"

Linus grabbed the front of the bully's shirt and shook him furiously. "Janice has leukemia, cement head! That's cancer. Have you ever heard of cancer? She's been in the hospital. She's had chemotherapy to help her get better and it made her hair fall out. Does that make you happy? Would you like to go through what she's gone through? Think about it, or don't you ever think about anything?"

Linus and Janice turned to walk away. As they did, the boy picked up the cap and said very sheepishly, "I'm sorry." Then he suddenly brightened. "Hey, it really is a nice cap," he said.

At school, some of the other students in her class were talking about the extra attention that Janice was now getting.

"See," one whispered to another. "The teacher is always being extra nice to Janice. How does she get away with it?"

All day Linus defended her, of course. "You don't know what you're talking about. If she gets special treatment, it's because she's been sick."

Early that evening, Charlie Brown was sitting in his favorite chair reading when Snoopy opened the door and walked into the room with a long extension cord. He unplugged the lamp next to Charlie Brown and plugged in his own extension cord. Immediately, all of the Christmas tree lights that he had strung around his doghouse lit up, and he now had the most beautifully decorated home in the neighborhood.

At the same time, Linus was taking the Christmas gift he had bought for Janice over to her house. When he knocked on the door, a little girl answered.

"Hi," said Linus. "Is Janice home? I'm Linus. I sit in front of her at school."

"I'm Janice's little sister. She's not home. She had to go back for one of her treatments, but I think she'll come home again tomorrow."

Another girl joined them at the door and said, "Hi. What's going on? I'm Janice's older sister."

"This is Linus," said the little girl. "He brought Janice a present."

"Another present?" said the older sister. "Everyone brings Janice something. She gets more presents than the two of us together, and we have to be so careful around her. We can't even get the chicken pox. If we did, she would catch it from us and it would be really bad for her. Actually, she's becoming a real nuisance."

"You don't really mean that, do you?" said Linus. "She's your sister."

"Well, I don't know. I guess not. It's just that we've been feeling a little left out lately since Janice got sick."

The two sisters took Linus's gift inside and placed it with all of the others under the tree. "She sure gets a lot of presents, though."

"Well," said Linus, "maybe that's a way for people to show they hope she gets well."

After the holidays, Janice's classroom desk remained empty. The weeks went by, and the weather grew warmer. Finally, one early spring morning, Janice returned to the bus stop.

"Janice, you're back!" said Linus. "How do you feel?"

"Much better, thank you. I can't believe the snow is melting. I've been inside so long."

Charlie Brown said, "We're all glad you're back. It was sad seeing your empty desk when you were gone for treatment."

"I missed being in school," said Janice.

A few weeks later at the school playground, Linus led Janice to the swings that had finally been put up again after the long winter. "See," he said. "They're up! The swings are up again!"

"I have a surprise for you, Linus," said Janice, as she crawled up onto the swing. "But, first, push me. Push me, Linus!"

Carefully, he pulled her back and gave her a big push.

"Higher!" shouted Janice. "Push me higher!"

He pushed her harder, and she began to swing up and up, and Linus shouted, "What's the surprise?"

As the swing rose high into the morning sunlight, Janice tilted her head back and let the wind catch under the bill of her pink cap. Suddenly, it flew off, and her beautiful blonde hair swirled free behind her.

Linus shouted out, then yelled a cheer and Janice laughed, and the cap she'd worn all winter long, the cap she wouldn't need to wear any longer, fell quietly to the ground. Janice was back!

Glossary for Parents

Acute Occurring suddenly or over a short period of time.

Benign Tumor A noncancerous growth that does not spread to other parts of the body. Outlook for recovery is favorable with treatment.

Bone Marrow The spongy material that fills the cavities of the bones and is the substance in which many of the blood elements are produced. In order to determine the condition of the marrow, a doctor may take a small sample from one of the bones in the chest, hip, spine, or leg. Such examinations are performed with the help of a local anesthesia.

Cancer A general term for about 100 diseases characterized by uncontrolled, abnormal growth of cells. The resulting mass, or tumor, can invade and destroy surrounding normal tissues. Cancer cells from the tumor can spread through the blood or lymph (the clear fluid that bathes body cells) to start new cancers in other parts of the body (metastases).

Carcinogen A chemical or other agent that causes cancer.

CAT Scan (Computerized Axial Tomography) Diagnostic X-ray procedure in which a computer is used to generate a three-dimensional image.

Chemotherapy Treatment with anti-cancer drugs.

Chronic A term that is used to describe a disease of long duration or one that is progressing slowly.

Immune System The body's system of defenses against disease, composed of certain white blood cells and antibodies. Antibodies are protein substances that react against bacteria and other harmful material.

Intravenous The administration of a drug or fluid directly into a vein.

Malignant Tending to become progressively worse; in the case of cancer, it implies ability to invade, disseminate, and actively destroy surrounding tissue.

Oncologist A physician who specializes in cancer.

Oncology the study of physical, chemical, and biological properties and features of cancer.

Radiation Therapy Treatment using high-energy radiation from X-ray machines, cobalt, radium, or other sources.

Relapse The reappearance of a disease after a period when symptoms have lessened or ceased.

Remission The decrease or disappearance of cancer symptoms. Also the period in which this occurs.

Tumor Any abnormal growth or mass.

X-Rays High-energy radiation used in high doses to treat cancer or in low doses to diagnose the disease.

Glossary courtesy of the National Cancer Society
and the U.S. Department of Health and Human Services.